MY PROTECTIVE BIKER

An ABDL MM Biker Romance

Jerry Hastings
Michael Levi

CONTENTS

CHAPTER 1

Gary

I didn't want to have to think about my life, and I didn't want to remember that I dropped out of college. And that wasn't enough for me, either.

I was now walking in the desert, trying to pretend I wasn't looking like a fool. I had a falling out with my father. He raised me all by himself.

When I was little, I thought he was an amazing man and we did everything together. But he raised me to become a man molded by his ideas.

Drinking, picking up random girls in the streets, and having fights with people that were once his friends - his life was loose like that and he was disappointed I grew up to become someone more responsible.

Holding a backpack in my hand, I was hating how heavy it was. And it wasn't even that heavy, to begin with. It was just feeling like that because I was thirsty, despising the fact I didn't have a new diaper to change the one I was wearing, and also better shoes. The pavement had long devoured the soles of the ones I was wearing.

I tried not to think too much about that and focused on my destination. Well, calling it that would be generous. All I knew was that I needed to add as much distance as possible between me and my father. He was still hunting down for me and it was his way of showing he cared.

But he didn't care when he landed that punch in my face. My teeth and cheek were still stinging.

Cars and trucks were speeding up past me, not bothering at all to slow down and check up on me. As a little, I knew about the dangers of meeting strangers I didn't know anything about and was kind of glad no one was pulling over for me.

Walking as if my feet weighed like 1000 tons, I didn't bother to lift my head when a truck zipped past me and the driver shouted names. He was just another fat loser with a protruding beer belly. I couldn't care less about him.

My phone was beginning to buzz and annoy me. I did have some friends and I was pretty sure they were worried sick. After all, they thought I was going to see them after work.

And work... It wasn't something I thought often about anymore. Cleaning up toilets sucked ass and I had to hide the fact I was a little from everyone. After all, what would my bosses think if they found out? They'd kick me out and I'd be lucky if I got paid what was due.

Shaking my head, my legs wobbled and I almost lost my footing after finding out I couldn't go on for much longer.

The distance between Los Angeles and Las Vegas was too long for me to walk there. What was I thinking when I made that choice? I was out of my mind and it showed.

Dropping my ass on the pavement, I watched as the sun shone in full brightness on my face. I lifted my arm and shaded my eyes while I admired the beautifulness of the sky. It was bright blue and I couldn't see any clouds.

It was the middle of the summer season and temperatures were still rising. My diaper was pressing against my hips and butt, feeling soaked. I had terrible dreams last night that were going to haunt me for the rest of my life.

As a guy in his early twenties, I was fearful that I was going to end up alone. It wasn't enough that I was born gay, but I was also a little. That made my partner options limited and it was one of the reasons why I hated myself. Kind of. I wasn't going to say that I hated myself that much.

I was wondering what was going to happen now when a truck started to approach me. I didn't think much of it and focused on the tumbleweed rolling in the distance. I wished I was kind of like it, with nothing to worry about other than where the wind was going to take me next.

Focusing on that, I noticed that the truck was pulling over. Could it be that someone was finally taking pity on me? I looked like your average young guy and people knew I shouldn't be by the road in the middle of a desert. If I had really thought it was possible to get from Los Angeles to Las Vegas on foot, then I'd been a fool.

No wonder that the trucker was pulling over.

I didn't focus on that much and remained where I was. The ground was hot and was burning through my jeans, but that was okay. I'd been through worse things before.

Just when I was thinking I might as well stand up and leave this place, the truck finished pulling over. All the parts and hinges in it were creaking like this was its last stop and that it was on its last legs. Last legs for a truck. Now that was a funny thought.

I chuckled as the guy shifted over until he was sitting on the other seat of the truck. It looked massive and kind of a little menacing.

He looked like a boomer through and through. He had a thick beard, a greasy face, and a shiny, bald head. I tried not to focus too much on those things as I remembered that he didn't choose to be that way. Well, for most of the things I mentioned, he didn't have a choice anyway.

"Are you lost or something?" He asked, his mouth barely moving. I didn't know why I focused on that, but the thought crossed my mind and I was hating myself for it. My diaper was smelling and I was kind of not feeling like getting in his truck. What if he noticed the smell and kicked me out of it? I supposed that at least he would take me to Las Vegas. And, from there, after meeting a friend of mine, who didn't know I was coming, I'd find a way to restart my life.

"Something like that. I'm going to Las Vegas."

"It's a long way there. You wanna a ride?" He asked and even though I didn't have any reason to think he had I'll intentions, the thought still crossed my mind. I had a good heart and I didn't want to think that he was planning on hurting me. Still, stranger danger and that sort of thing.

He looked friendly enough, but I was just not too sure about hopping in there.

"No, thanks." I was happy that I was finally making a decision and hoping I could transport that to other aspects of my life. Most of the time, I couldn't make a decision and that always ruined everything for me.

"No? Are you sure? I'm not going to leave until after you've thought a little better about that."

His eyes were looking fierce all of a sudden, and I was realizing that I might be making a mistake. I shouldn't even have told him I was going to Las Vegas.

I shifted my eyes from side to side and couldn't find a police car coming this way. I didn't like them at all, especially given that some were pretty brutal when they had to deal with guys like me. They couldn't bully the real, dangerous criminals, so they focused on mistreating smaller men.

Just the thought of having to depend on one of them to save my ass now was churning my stomach.

"Yeah, and it's still no. I'm not going. I want to stay here and doing nothing"

"Well, that's not going to happen," he said, shifting over to the other door and opening it. I shot up and considered running away, only to find out that my legs were in too much pain.

I couldn't run, and that guy was coming for me. He was going to kidnap me.

"Now, what do you think you're doing?" He said, rounding the front of his truck faster than I thought he could, latching a hand around my forearm and dragging me with him.

"What are you doing? Leave me alone!" I shouted, realizing that this was going from bad to worse in a matter of seconds. Not only was he going to kidnap me, that also meant he had other plans in mind.

I wasn't a child anymore, but I was pretty sure that he was still looking at me as if I were one. He might be a rapist, a child abuser, and all other kinds of things, and I didn't want to have anything to do with him. I knew that I was in danger and that I needed to get out of here right away.

Cars and other trucks continued to speed up past us, without a care in the world. I didn't think that they were bad people, but they were too absorbed in what they were doing to notice what was happening. That was how society was like nowadays. Nobody cared about other people anymore.

He dragged me to the other side of the front of the truck, opened the door, and shoved me inside it. I tried to fight back, kicking the air and punching his face, but that only further annoyed him.

"Stop doing that, you little piece of shit," he groaned, fisting his hand and landing a solid punch in my face.

I couldn't see anything, blacking out and hoping that he was no child abductor. I didn't want to find out where he was going to take me.

And now, most of all, I was hoping that someone was going to save me.

CHAPTER 2

Jim

It was dark outside and all we could see was the desert. We were heading to Los Vegas, the loud rumbling noise of our bikes stealing the attention of the drivers. They were driving cars and trucks, which couldn't match the speed and flexibility of our bikes. Sitting on my Guardian was one of the best things in the world and, despite having had a terrible experience with a girl, I couldn't imagine myself ever leaving this life.

A couple of feet in front of me were Terry and Ramon. They were the president and the vice-president of the Spectral Rats MC. The lower parts of their leather jackets were flying in the air as we continued to speed up, knowing that this part of the road between the two cities wasn't well policed.

Ramon was with little Lucas, and they were considering settling down and living their life alone. After spending so much time with my buddies, that possibility was alluring to me. What I wouldn't do right now to be doing that, too.

We could see Las Vegas in the distance, all the lights from the Strip alluring me. This was the kind of life we had to live now. After Ramon's last partner turned out to be a rat, we couldn't imagine ourselves ever having another building for our club.

Just thinking about that made me remember how much that sucked. We loved that building near downtown Houston where we could have all the privacy we needed. Not to mention that there it was much easier to find more members for the club. We weren't running short on citizens, but we couldn't be on the run forever.

The rumbling of the engine of the Guardian was comforting, my grip certain. We were dodging past cars and trucks alike, always keeping our formation. The president and the vice-president always had to take the lead, and I was a little behind them.

They had their littles now. They were living a happy, different life that I didn't know much about. Of course, living with them meant I was always going to know a little about ABDL and that sort of thing.

I was bi, but I wouldn't say if caring for someone pretending to be a child was the right thing for me. I tried keeping an open mind and I considered myself one of their friends, but there was still something about it I couldn't quite put my finger on.

I reminded myself that I could never tell them those things, and focused on the road ahead.

My Guardian was cutting through the traffic like a hot knife through butter, and I was already washing away all the worrisome thoughts in my mind. I'd been with that girl all of my life, and I never thought she'd end up choosing someone else. It happened after she found out about the real me. She thought that I wasn't right for her, and when I mentioned that we were going to have to leave Houston, she flipped.

Seconds later, my eyes caught sight of something unusual by the road and I sped up forward, signaling with my hand for everyone to pull over. Terry and Ramon exchanged glances as if they were asking themselves what was going on, and they were soon going to find out what was making my heart race.

I'd spotted a body lying on the pavement by the road, and I couldn't have ignored it. It was the body of a young man, who was most likely in his early twenties. He had a backpack with him, and his clothes were raggedy and full of holes.

Whatever happened with him, it had been bad and it was driving up the caring part of me I didn't think I had. Not for someone I didn't know anything about, at least.

Terry and Ramon pulled over as they finally noticed the man lying on the ground. My heart was in pain for him and I already was finding myself wanting to kick the shit out of the asshole who did that.

I put my bike at an angle and took off my helmet, putting it under my arm. I walked up to him and my heart skipped a beat when I realized that he'd passed out. He couldn't be more than 25 and it hurt me to see someone in this condition. Once again, I promised myself that I would beat the shit out of the asshole who did this.

"What happened here?" I mumbled to myself after squatting and putting my helmet on the ground. The wind was swirling around me, kicking up dirt while everyone else also stopped to check out who this little guy was.

I put my finger on the side of his neck and was relieved when I found out he was still alive. I thought that someone left here to rot in the middle of nowhere would be dead 9 times out of ten, but this appeared to be one of the lucky ones in that assumption.

I shifted my eyes down as Terry came up to me. Their littles were waiting for them on their bikes and I knew that they weren't allowing them to come over here until they were sure it was safe for them.

His hand moved over to the back of his pants. I didn't think much of that until he grabbed a small part of something that was protruding. I wasn't stupid and soon realized what it was.

"It's a diaper. He's a little too," he murmured, and just as he finished saying that, the little guy started to open his eyes. Eyelids went up, down, and then up again. He was tired and I could see that he was famished. The first thought that was coming into my mind was that I needed to get him out of here as soon as possible. And the other thought that followed it, about having lost our HQ, was making my blood boil.

I couldn't stay here doing nothing, noticing as this man started to wake up.

He turned his head until he was looking at me, and at that moment, something started to permeate my mind. It had been a long time since I felt anything for anybody, and that guy was doing just that to me. He wasn't meaning to, but it was still happening, and I couldn't control it.

"We need to get him to Las Vegas. It's the only place where we can find a room for him, or set up camp," I affirmed, already admitting to myself that putting him in a tent wouldn't be enough. He needed to be taken to a proper room, have a good bath, and then sleep well in a king-sized bed.

Ramon shifted his eyes toward me and nodded. He was a little more understanding, and looked happy that the young man was already awake.

"What happened?" He asked, and his voice was sweet and gentle. I felt like I was finding the love of my life again, even though that didn't make any sense. Why would I be thinking something like that of him when I didn't know him at all?

"You are going to have to explain that one to us," I affirmed while putting him in my arms and taking him to the Guardian. On other occasions, when he was stronger and less hungry, he would be fighting back and struggling, but now it was the Daddy side of me that was taking over.

My bike was big enough to keep him in the front of it. I put him carefully in there while everyone else got back on their bikes. I started to twist the throttle until the engine was roaring to life. After we took off, I noticed that he was already falling asleep while resting his head in the crook of my neck.

I didn't know what was about him, but just being near him this way was calming my racing heart in a way I never thought possible. My eyes were set on the goal ahead, which was getting to Las Vegas and finding a good apartment room for us. I didn't usually splurge, but now I was already thinking about using my savings to get him something nicer, which would warm up his heart.

CHAPTER 3

Gary

I found myself lying in a bed, already panicking that my dad had found me out and taken me here. I shifted my eyes from side to side and realized that that couldn't be the case. The room was different from my old one, it had a distinct smell in it, and voices were coming from the other side of a wall, which were reminding me of the men that saved me not too long ago.

I couldn't believe that had happened. It was all coming back to me. That trucker had kidnapped me, beat the shit out of me, and left me to rot by the road. I was feeling like shit, even though the blanket I was lying underneath was warm and comfortable. Whoever had put me here, they cared about me.

I shifted my eyes when the door opened all of a sudden. I didn't know if he knew that I was already waking up, but the timing couldn't have been more perfect. My stomach was rumbling and my throat was dry.

He was holding a bedside table in his hands and was just taking it towards me when his eyes noticed mine. "Oh, you're already awake," he said, something spreading over his face and making me feel something for him I never thought possible.

He had short, sharp brown hair, and emerald green eyes. His skin was a little olive-ish and there was something different about his accent. I couldn't know this for sure without asking, but it looked like he was Italian.

I tried not to think about those things much. Even though they made my dick harden a little, they didn't have any importance right now.

Someone else stepped through the door when he realized that I was already waking up. He stopped in his tracks and put his right hand on the frame of the door. He looked a little older and a little more certain about himself than the guy that was nearer me. It wasn't that the latter lacked self-esteem, but that something was going on in his mind. And me being curious me, I couldn't help but wonder what that was.

"Oh, I didn't know you were already awake. I'm Terry," he said with a confident smile, walking up to me and holding out his hand. I took it and we shook hands. His grip was firm but warm.

The other guy turned his head and looked at him with jealousy in his eyes. I didn't know what was going on in his head, but his being jealous of a simple handshake made me blush.

"I'm Gary," I said, and he nodded.

There was a moment of silence that was broken only by his next words.

"If you need anything, you know where to find me," he said and turned around after speaking some more with me. It wasn't that he was in a hurry or anything like that. He did show that he wasn't used to being in a hotel, but he didn't want to let that get in the way of his being.

The first took off and left me all alone with the other guy in his room. The door closed and I was left in a very uncomfortable situation where I didn't know what to say. I supposed that introductions were more than critical at this moment, but I didn't feel like opening my mouth.

It looked like he didn't know how to act in front of a guy like me. He looked tough, was tall, and his biceps were as big as my head, but he still had his shy side, and that was enough to make me feel a bit more at ease with him.

He walked up to me, put the bedside dinner table in front of me, and sat down on a chair by the bed.

"I'm Jim, and I guess I don't need to tell you this. I'm a biker from the Spectral Rats MC. We found you lying on a road."

I looked down, not focusing on the food. It looked good and it couldn't be much better, but that wasn't the problem that was permeating my mind. Rather, it was all the memories those words were shooting into my mind. I was remembering everything.

Well, not every little detail of it, but it was still enough to make me shed a tear. It rolled down my cheek and my heart was feeling tighter. I wanted to punch myself for letting that happen. I should have been stronger.

"A man... He kidnapped me. I thought he was going to do things I'd rather not mention, but I feel okay."

"Are you sure? Because, if something happened, I want you to tell me everything."

"No, I don't think he did anything more than that. He disappeared and left me lying there. Something must have happened which changed his mind."

He leaned over until he was putting his hand on mine.

"You don't need to let that keep hurting you. Whatever happens from now on, I'm going to be by your side."

"Thanks, Jim," I said with a smile on my face. There was no denying that he hit every imaginable checkbox that made him look like a Daddy, even though I didn't think he was. There was a sense of understanding in his face regarding my current condition, but that was about it. When it came to being someone responsible, he was one of the best.

"You don't know anything else about him?" He asked, his hand feeling comfortable and making me feel like I could trust him. I wasn't going to say I did, but the thought was still in my mind. I wanted to find someone that would be with me at all times and tell me that I was following the right path.

His hand was also pretty big and it was turning me on. I wanted to tell him those things, but the shyness in me was preventing me from doing that.

He took his hand off mine as I responded, "No, I was... just walking."

I didn't say anything else as I moved my head until I was looking down again. His eyes were attentive and they were pretty to look at, but it was also like they were trying to probe into my thoughts. That wasn't too bad, but I was still not feeling ready enough to be talking about those things.

"Just walking? You know that you don't need to hide anything from me."

And how was I going to tell him I didn't quite fully trust him yet? As far as I knew, he was just a stranger who happened to save me. And even though he looked a lot more friendly than that trucker, I didn't know if I was feeling ready to tell him anything about what happened before he met me.

"I'm not hiding anything from you. It's just… difficult."

He reclined in his chair, putting his hands on his lap and looking at me with forceful eyes. But they weren't forceful in a way that made me feel like talking to him. I could see myself trusting him one day… I just didn't know if now was the right moment for that.

Not to mention the whole thing about me being a little and him being a biker. I didn't think that what we were having now would ever become more than what it already was. I was happy he'd saved me… I just wasn't the kind of person that dove into something and didn't look back.

In fact, I was already thinking about all the implications of this meeting with him. I was hoping that he wasn't thinking we were going to do… something else tonight.

There was another moment of silence that was only broken by his next words.

"You are a little, aren't you?"

My heart skipped a beat, and for a moment I didn't know what to say. He just threw that out in the air like it was the most common thing in the world to say. I supposed that him finding me when I was unconscious and taking me here might have allowed him to notice my diaper, but still… I never thought that someone would just say what he did.

I opened my mouth and closed it over and over. I looked like a goldfish, and I couldn't even try to hide that.

Jim opened a shy smile and looked at me with understanding

in his eyes.

"I'm sorry. I didn't mean to make you feel like that."

"It's not that. I just thought… It all came out all of a sudden. I didn't think you were going to figure it out so easily."

"It's the diaper, and you're not the only little in our club."

"What?" The question popped up in my mind all of a sudden, and I just had to ask him.

"There are two littles just like you living with us. I know our life is difficult, especially riding around on bikes and not having a permanent home, but it is what it is."

I couldn't wrap my head around it. Here was this man, who was at least a decade older than me, telling me that he knew about my littleness and that other people in his MC were like me. Was I living in some kind of dream now? Because nothing of this made any sense.

He widened his smile and said, "You don't need to look like that. It's no secret to me."

"It's just that… I've been keeping it hidden from everyone this whole time."

"Well, not anymore. You don't need to keep it hidden from me any longer."

His smile was an easy one and it was warming up my heart. I could actually find myself trusting him, but that was the thing. Trust wasn't something that came easy anymore in this day and age. After finding out I couldn't even trust my father, I was always going to be skeptical.

He put his hand on mine again, looking at my eyes with determination. "If you need someone to speak about everything that happened, you can talk to me."

And I couldn't hold them back anymore. Tears started to pour out and roll down my cheeks. I was crying in front of a stranger who was the first person that was showing me compassion. I'd been walking in the desert for so long I thought that all the people in the world were assholes.

"I'm sorry," he said, putting me in his arms and allowing my head to rest in the crook of his neck again. I was still sitting on the bed and it was kind of uncomfortable hugging him this way, but there wasn't much that could be done about that.

I needed someone to be hugging right now, and he was the only one available.

I didn't think about anything else as the tears stopped coming out. I was opening up to a man I didn't know much about. I knew his name, but that was about it, and it was still so good to be hugging him right now.

I could even hear the beating of his heart. It was comforting, and he was acting like the Daddy I'd been looking for this whole time. This was what ABDL was all about to me. Having someone that cared about me and didn't try to hide that.

I fell asleep while I was still crying, and I didn't feel ashamed at all.

CHAPTER 4

Jim

I didn't think he would just break down the way he did, much less that he would fall asleep in my arms without taking a bite of his food. I didn't prepare it, but part of me was still hoping for that approval from him – that he liked it and wanted more.

I couldn't hide the feeling that was sprouting up in me. I was acting like the Daddy he'd been looking for his whole life, and it was good to be having that effect on him.

I put him under the blanket again and allowed him the time he needed to sleep now. He looked so angelic and I felt like kissing him. Not giving him a kiss on his lips or anything of the sort, but just... kissing his forehead and telling him that he was someone special.

I didn't think too much about that and picked up the bedside dinner table. I put it on top of the dresser in the room and wondered if he was going to wake up feeling better. Even if he didn't trust me, that was the thought that was in my mind. I just wanted to see him well.

I didn't think he was going to sleep for long. He'd already slept for hours and now should just be taking a short nap.

I was walking to the door when I heard him groaning and opening his eyes again. That surprised me, as I didn't think his nap was going to be that short. Something in me was telling me that was happening because he had a couple more things he wanted to tell me.

"I... also had a falling out with my father. He lives alone now and he doesn't like who I am. He thinks I'm weird and that I should be more like him."

Hearing him saying that, it helped me feel more connected to him. I didn't have a bad relationship with my parents. In fact, they both died when I was still a child. I was raised as an orphan, which was something about me I treasured. It toughened me up like nothing could have.

I couldn't help but rush over to him, putting my arms around him and hugging him with the strength of a bear. He melted in my arms and, for a moment, I felt the beating of his heart.

"Thank you. You're very kind," he said, and his eyes were twinkling like he was finding the calling of his life.

There was something I was readying myself to tell him. I didn't know how he was going to take it, but I supposed it couldn't be delayed anymore.

I walked up to the closet and opened it. This hotel room had it and also the dresser. Inside it was the diaper I'd bought for him. It took me a while to find a good one. Since he was an adult, I couldn't have bought one of the smaller ones. I bought a geriatric diaper and I was hoping he was going to like it. He should, considering it was better than the soiled thing he had on.

He didn't say he had incontinence, but the smell was in the air and it was making me think he had that.

I turned around, holding out the diaper. His eyes went wide as soon as he noticed them. I was finally realizing that this was indeed happening. I was going to diaper him. Or change his diaper, more like. I just couldn't leave him with his soiled, smelly diaper.

"You're not... actually thinking about doing that, are you?" He questioned, and I could only widen my smile. I was really doing this. I was changing the diaper of an adult, which was something I thought would never happen in my life.

"Yes, I am. And out of that blanket you are coming! I can't change you when you still have it covering you," I said, feeling my dick hardening. One would think we were a club of hardened bikers, and that this was one of the last things one of us would be doing one day. Little did they know that, after watching this happening so many times with Ramon and Terry, I already knew a thing or two about it.

Gary didn't push his blanket off him. I grabbed it and pulled it until I had full access to his body. He still had all of his clothes on, including his jeans and raggedy shirt. Just looking at those things was making me feel so sorry for him. He shouldn't be having to go through this, and he needed a caretaker now more than ever.

I pulled down the zipper of his pants and helped him out of them. His eyes were still looking at this with a surprise gleam in them, but it looked like he was already getting used to it.

"I never thought that this would happen today," he murmured more to himself than to me, and suddenly I felt like putting a pacifier in his mouth. It wasn't that I wanted to shut him up or anything of the sort, but that I was pretty sure it would make him feel better.

Not thinking about that much, I pulled up his shirt and took it off him. Depositing it on top of the jeans, which I was also going to have to throw away, I proceeded to scan his body from bottom to top with my eyes.

The connection I was feeling with him was intense. I wanted him, and my cock wanted him even more so. Still, I was kind of not thinking about having sex with him yet. I didn't think it was the right time yet.

Not to mention we didn't know each other well yet...

His diaper was reeking even worse now than before, and I couldn't wait until it was gone. Remembering that just putting a new diaper on him wasn't enough, I proceeded to the dresser and, from the top of it, I picked up a box of baby wipes and a bottle of talcum.

I still felt like this was something utterly new to me, that I would never be doing this if I hadn't met him, but it was okay. I wasn't letting those thoughts ruin the moment.

I disconnected the straps of his diaper and pulled it down, letting him lift his butt so that he was helping me. I didn't know what was going on in his mind, but he was blushing. He looked so cute when he was blushing.

I supposed he should take a bath before having his diaper changed, but I didn't want to change what we were already doing.

Not thinking too much about that, I plucked out some baby wipes and started to slide them over his butt. His skin was smooth and very sensitive. It didn't take me too long to realize that he was also going to need perfume or at least something to make him smell a little better until we got around to... bathing him.

Could that happen, too? Could I bathe him? I didn't know if he was ready to take that step yet.

Sliding another pair of baby wipes on his butt, I noticed his dick hardening. It was pretty small, especially for someone his age. He was turned on and couldn't hide that. Blushing, he was making me feel like kissing him right away. It was so bad we didn't know each other that well yet.

I finished cleaning up his bubble butt and proceeded to apply some talcum. It should work not only to make him smell better, but also to keep his skin protected. The diaper could sting his skin, and the last thing I wanted was him thinking that I didn't care about him. I did, quite a lot.

"Lift your butt again... little one," I said, noticing that the words were coming naturally out of my mouth. It was like this was what I'd been looking for all of my life, even though I'd always thought that couldn't be the case.

He obeyed and I slid the diaper underneath him. It was a little sad that it wasn't colorful and didn't have other fancy things, but that was okay. Part of me was hoping this was only our first time and that, in the future, he would allow me to change his diaper again.

I tried not to think too much about those things, focusing on doing this right. Living for so long with Terry and Ramon, I'd already learned a couple of things. I should know how to do this right. The only problem with that was doing it without feeling my heart so tight. I was sweating bullets, and that wasn't even the beginning of it.

He was looking at me while his small cock was still a little stiff.

After putting the diaper underneath him, I connected the straps and secured it. I felt like patting the front of it, but only didn't do so because I was still sweating. My heart was racing, and I was hoping he liked his new diaper.

"So-"

"It's perfect, Daddy!" He said loudly and with a happy smile on his face. Jumping off the bed, he swung his arms around me and hugged me with all of his strength. He wasn't heavy, but the way he did that still made me stumble.

"Woah there, calm down," I said, but I still put my hand on his back and started to caress it. I was loving our bonding, and it was the best thing ever we were doing since he woke up.

I was loving that he was hugging me now like this, but it happened out of nowhere. It caught me off guard.

The combination of his littleness, his body being so cute and small, and him hugging me like this was making me feel so turned on. My body was getting hotter, and I couldn't hide that.

When he moved his head backward, he started to look at me with kindness, compassion, and love in his eyes. That was it. That was what was happening, and I was falling in love with him. After seeing Ramon and Terry having the time of their lives living with their littles, I found out that I was seeking the same thing.

"You do realize I don't know anything about littles, right?" I asked, putting my hand on his cheek and feeling the softness of it. It was unlike anything I'd felt before. It was even better than the cheeks of my ex.

"But how couldn't you, when you changed my diaper like that and is making me feel so much better?"

I couldn't help but smile, approaching my head and kissing him. It was the best kiss of my life. I'd been only with girls before meeting him, and I never thought I'd be kissing another man so soon.

He didn't know how to kiss properly. It was quite awkward, but he was still doing his best. And I was soon realizing that I was going to have to direct the kiss.

I was sliding my tongue into his mouth, and it was the best

feeling ever. My whole body was resonating with the heat of this moment, and I couldn't imagine myself doing anything different right now.

After pressing my lips against his and rubbing them for what felt like hours, I finally ended the kiss with a sense of emptiness in my heart. Nevertheless, that feeling didn't last long until I lied down with him in the bed, after closing the door of his room.

I thought that this plan would never pop up in my mind, but now it already was. I could already imagine myself getting married to someone like him and settling down. I didn't know how long it would take to make those things happen, but they were already deeply ingrained in my mind.

"You don't need to fear anything anymore," I said, hugging him while I covered ourselves up in the bed. I loved the fact I was finally sleeping with someone else again, and I couldn't imagine myself having a bad night's sleep tonight, like all the other times before today.

I loved Gary, and I couldn't hide that.

CHAPTER 5

Gary

This roadside diner was fantastic. The people inside it, the motorcycles parked in front, and nothing else to admire in terms of views other than the infinite desert - it all mesmerized me. We were outside Las Vegas and after finding my Daddy, I wasn't thinking about going back there any time soon.

We got to cross through The Strip and it was pretty cool seeing all the lights and people losing money in their gambling ventures, but I couldn't imagine myself living there for more than a day. It was a cool and very touristic city, but that was all there was to it.

I was sitting in the booth of the diner and my daddy was in front of me. We had just finished making our orders and my stomach was rumbling because of the smell in the air. It was so great, and it reminded me of the time when I could still enjoy some decent home cooking.

The diner was packed. All the bikers from the Spectral Rats MC were in here, sitting in their booths and waiting for their orders, too. I had already befriended some of them. The two other littles that they had in the club were just like me. They were a little different, to be honest, but I still felt connected to them.

"How are you liking the place?" My Daddy asked, keeping both of his hands on the table between us. He looked as imperious and protective as before, and I felt safe with him.

"It's great!" And it really was. It had been such a long time since my real dad took me to a place like this one. The environment wasn't just cozy, but it was also very friendly for someone like me. I could look around and pretend that nobody was staring at me. That happened all the time in many other places, but it was different here. It was like everyone sitting in the diner was already accepting me, even though they didn't know me.

The door to the diner opened and my spine got stiff all of a sudden. That face, that body, and those eyes. I had seen him before and I knew who they belonged to. Of all the times I thought I would eventually end up seeing him again, this wasn't it.

He turned his head and widened his eyes when he noticed me seated in the booth. Daddy noticed what was going on with me and grabbed my hand.

"Is something the matter? What's going on?" He asked, worry spreading in his voice. I wanted to tell him that it didn't have anything to do with him, but that was easier said than done. My whole body was too stiff, and my heart was speeding up.

The other men walked over until he was standing beside us, saying with some hardness in his voice, "What is the meaning of this? What are you doing with this man?"

How was I going to explain this without feeling like trash? I couldn't and it was showing.

Jim stood up, looking a little taller than my dad. And after everything that happened, I couldn't keep calling him my real dad. He was Paul. Just Paul, and nothing else to me.

"He is with me now."

Jim looked imposing and menacing. He had tattoos all over his thick arms, and the patch in the front of his leather jacket was showing he wasn't the kind of man to be messed around with.

"What do you mean he is with you? I've been looking for him this whole time. He's my son and I'm taking him back."

Paul showing up here was sprouting up all kinds of memories in my mind. I didn't want to remember them and, yet, they were still making me wonder if what I was doing was the right thing.

It just didn't make sense. Jim was a biker and he was having a relationship with a little like me? What was I thinking was going to come out of that?

We didn't make anything official yet, but Paul's unwanted presence was still yanking me back to my old reality. I was already thinking that I wasn't right for Jim and that our relationship was going to end in pain.

"No. He isn't your son anymore. You hurt him," Jim growled, making me feel shivers shooting down my spine. I knew that he was very protective of me and a little hotheaded, but for the love of god, I didn't want him to pick a fight.

"What do you mean he isn't my son anymore?" Paul wasn't backing down or letting Jim's threats intimidate him. He was fighting back and the interior of the diner was already growing tense.

The other bikers were standing up. Carson and Lucas were already sneaking out as they didn't want any part of what was happening.

"You punched him and he had to walk out of his house. Do you think that's something you could ever forgive yourself for?"

They were on the verge of bumping their chests against each other. Paul didn't look as menacing and tough as Jim, but he was still no slouch. He might lose in a fight but that didn't mean he wouldn't be able to hurt Jim and I didn't want to let that happen.

"I'm going to call the police if you don't walk out and leave me alone with my son."

I wasn't going to deny that seeing Jim doing all this just for me was cool, but it was also making my palms sweat. He was protective, but when it came to defending me, nothing could stand in his way.

Paul turned his head around, noticing that he was surrounded. Even if he was thinking about letting go of it and walking out, the damage had already been done.

Had the relationship started much before now, it would be okay. I would feel stronger about it and not let anything ruin it, but Paul was already making me think I could never be the right man for Jim.

My hand looked for my paci and I put it in my mouth. I couldn't go on for another second without suckling on it. I needed it now like the fish needed water. It was the only way of making myself feel calmer.

Paul turned his head until he was looking at me. The sense of disapproval that appeared in his eyes was unmistakable. He didn't like that I had a pacifier in my mouth. He was still thinking I should be more like him.

After noticing he was surrounded and that he couldn't hope to fight all of them at once, he turned his head to me again. My heart was speeding up and it was feeling tighter than before.

"Are you really sure about this, Gary? If they are keeping you against your will, then don't hesitate to tell me everything. I'll call the police now if I have to."

For a moment, I didn't know what to say. I felt that telling my father I wanted to remain with them was what would make me feel better, but the problem was doing that when so much of my life was hanging on this.

I didn't stand up. I couldn't face him head-on like Jim was. I was a little through and through, and that was never going to change.

I still took the pacifier out of my mouth and said, "Yes, I want to be with him and I don't want to come back."

His lower left eyelid twitched. He thought the answer was going to be different, even though I never gave any indications of that. I told him everything as it was. I was happy with Jim.

He tsked and walked out. The interior of the diner had grown intense during his stay, but people were already sitting back in their booths. Cutlery was clinking and people were talking again, and Jim was sitting back in our booth.

I didn't know if I could hold back the tears any longer. They were coming up and I felt the urge to cry. Far too many strong emotions shot through me when my father was here.

Jim, noticing that, shot up and grabbed me. He didn't put me in his arms like part of me was hoping he would, but he took me out of the diner. As for our orders, we were going to have to eat them another time.

And I didn't know if what was ruined could still be fixed.

There was a bench positioned right outside the diner, on the back side of it. We sat down on it and Jim put one arm around my shoulders. He pulled me until I was resting my body against him, and he was then murmuring something into my ear. I could almost not focus on the words, given all the things that were still filling up my mind.

"Shhh, I know that was quite a lot for you to process, but there's still no need to cry. I'm right here with you, and so is everyone else."

He grabbed my hand, picked the paci out of it, and then put it in my mouth. It was good and it was already slowing down my heart, but it was still not good enough to wash away all these horrible memories.

And I couldn't tell him what was really going on in my mind...

"I know, but..."

"But...?" He asked, moving his hand until he was putting it on my cheek and leading my head toward him, kissing me. His eyes were filled with worry. He never thought that this moment would come so soon.

His lips were like magic. I was loving how we were kissing, and I couldn't imagine myself doing anything different right now.

"It's just a lot for me to process." I was lying and I was hoping I was doing it right this time. I didn't want him to find out the truth about that.

"Don't worry. I'm going to make everything better."

Without asking me if I wanted it, he was pressing his lips to mine again and making me have mixed feelings. It was good to be feeling his hot breath, the warmth of his body, and his arms making me feel so safe again, but I was still questioning where our relationship was going to end.

We hadn't even had sex for the first time, and this was where all of this was leading to.

He slid his tongue into my mouth, making this moment feel even more special. His thumb was caressing over my cheek, and my body was melting more and more for him. Part of me felt like I couldn't go for a day without kissing him, and the rest of me, the larger part, was shouting that this was all a lie.

That, as soon as he came to his senses, he would think he was making a mistake.

He ended the kiss, our lips severing the connection and making me feel like there was something huge missing in me. I tried not to let it consume me, but it was true that the thought was still in my mind.

"There. Feeling better now?" He asked, and that was only making me feel worse. What if I hurt him by walking out? The thought was crossing my mind, and I didn't know what to do with it. All I knew was that I couldn't keep this up for much longer.

Making a decision now was more than necessary, and I needed to choose what was better for me.

When we stood up, he grabbed my hand and held it until we were walking back into the diner. One of the waitresses was already coming over with our food and, for a moment, I didn't have to think about anything.

I could focus only on the taste and the smell of those bacon strips.

CHAPTER 6

Gary

We rented another hotel room for the night. Well, just for tonight. He was opening the door and stepping into the room. Jim had an easy smile on his face and I knew he'd been preparing for tonight for a very long time. And I couldn't stop loving every aspect of that.

He was already undoing the first buttons of his shirt. My dick was hard and I was finally not thinking about all the things that worried me. This was a very singular moment where everything was going right for me.

My heart was beating so fast in my chest it was like it wanted to come out. I had felt his hard muscles before and I felt that this was the culmination of everything we'd been doing right. My father hadn't tried to find me again and even though I couldn't be sure about this right now, I was already suspecting that he'd called off the police investigation into my disappearance.

The trucker that had kidnapped me was now nothing more than a distant dream. I was pretty sure that Jim would love wiping the floor with him, but he couldn't do that without first finding out where it was that he lived.

Anyway, I wasn't thinking about those things when he finished undoing the last button of his shirt. Tonight was different. He wasn't wearing his leather jacket because he wanted to look more presentable to me, and I couldn't help but think that was a mistake. He didn't need to hide anything from me anymore, and he already looked pretty damn handsome as he was.

My dick was hard, and I didn't have my diaper on tonight. I wasn't his little right now, but his boyfriend, and I was loving every minute of that.

The room didn't have candles lighting it, but the lamps were still casting a warm glow in the environment. It was highlighting the best about his body and, right now, I was finally taking my first peek at it.

And, my goodness. It was like I was looking at a god. His muscles were big, round, and looked pretty hard, too. I was finding it hard not to be drooling from both sides of my mouth. My goal was only one – I wanted to feel all of him, and I couldn't help but imagine how big his dick was, too.

Not thinking too much about that, I drew in a short breath when he started to undo the belt of his pants. They fell to the floor when he gave it a little push. It was enough to bring it down, and now I was looking at a man that was too big for me.

That boner in his underwear that he couldn't hide at all...

The curves of his body were almost too perfect, and I couldn't imagine myself doing anything right now that wasn't admiring them. His skin was shiny and he looked almost like he was sweating, even though that couldn't be the case. He was in his natural environment, and the easy smile on his face was showing me that.

The tattoos on his body were making me lust over him more than I already was, and I found myself wishing he was driving his cock inside of me. I wondered how long it was going to take until he was doing that.

He raced over to me, jumping on the bed and dropping his body until he was right on top of me. His dick was hard and was tempting me to suck him off right now. The only reason why I wasn't doing that was that I didn't want to ruin any part of this moment.

I tried not to think too much about that, letting him seize my shoulders with his hands while the weight of his body sagged the bed. He made his lips fall until he was kissing me with fervor. And me not knowing the ins and outs of what sex was supposed to be like, I didn't know what I should be doing.

His hands were roaming over my body and he was using his fingers in ways I never thought possible. He knew how to knead my skin and when to apply the right amount of pressure with them.

My body was resonating with his when I dropped my hands on his back. It was big and I could feel his muscles working as he continued to land more and more kisses all over my body. They were hot and very wet, forcing me to also put my legs around the small of his back.

I was groaning and moaning, and not feeling any shame about that. I was finally going to lose my V-card, and it was the best thing that could be happening to me right now.

All I could hear was his ragged breathing and feel like his body was becoming bigger with each passing second. My dick was pulsing, and my mind was already asking itself how much longer it could keep going without shooting all of my come out.

All of a sudden, I felt something getting ripped off of me. I opened my eyes and found out that it was my underwear. Most of the time, I didn't use one, but tonight was a different occasion. I wanted to look and feel just right for him.

He was groaning and nibbling on my earlobe, finally moving his underwear down with his hands. It was at that moment I finally saw his dick for the first time, and it looked so big it might as well be more than the size of two. I didn't think that it could fit inside me at all. It was sending shivers down my spine.

"You don't need to worry. I'm going to be very gentle," he promised, lowering himself until he was kissing my pectorals and belly. His hands were all over me and loving me in ways I never thought possible. Applying just the right amount of pressure each time he was kneading my skin, it was as if this moment could never end.

And the best thing about that? I wanted that to happen in that manner.

I couldn't control myself as he finally moved until his cock was right in front of me. I opened my mouth and started to suck him off.

His balls were right in front of me and I couldn't help myself. I started to play with them, using my fingers in ways I thought he was going to like. He was moaning as he continued to stay still and gave me all the time I needed to worship him.

I thought of nothing in particular, just cherishing the heat of this moment, his beating heart, and loving it when he moved away from me. He wasn't stopping our sex, but he was taking it a step further and was now going to fuck me in ways I couldn't even imagine.

He smiled and turned me around. Walking towards the dresser, he opened one of the drawers and took something out of it. I could only imagine what it was as I couldn't open my eyes. He'd told me that, when he was to take my virginity, I was to keep them closed, and I couldn't help but obey every order of his.

I tried not to think about all the implications of my actions and focused on him. He was climbing up the bed again and putting himself right behind me. His hands opened one of the bottles and the smell of it, although faint, was still noticeable.

I shivered at the thought of him finally penetrating me, and I knew it wasn't going to take too long until that was happening.

He spread all the lube on his hands and started to smear the substance on my asscheeks. My butt was ready for him, and I couldn't wait until he was penetrating me.

Thinking about that only, it wasn't too surprising when he started to ease his dick inside of me. He was digging his fingers in my skin and was making sure I couldn't escape what was happening. And I wouldn't be doing that even if I was trying to.

His cock was too massive and waves of pain were shooting throughout my body. I felt like there was no end to it and when he reached the end of my rectum, he groaned and showed his disappointment. I didn't know what he was hoping he was going to do. He was too thick and long for me. I never thought he would manage to fit all of those inches inside.

Rolling his hips, he was soon pounding in and out of me, and I came several times. I was finally losing my virginity, and it was the best thing to be happening in my life. If there was a way to go back and make the choice of meeting him earlier, I'd be doing that right now 10 times out of 10.

He plopped down on the bed when he was finished, putting me in his arms and hugging me. I couldn't help but fall asleep, certain that tomorrow I was going to have to make a final choice.

When I fell in love with him, I never thought that things would be happening in this manner. And yet, they were.

✳   ✳   ✳

I was looking behind my shoulders and wondering if I was making the right choice. I was leaving him all by himself. Well, he wasn't really going to be all alone, but he was still going to look at it and think he'd made a mistake sometime in the past.

Adjusting my backpack so that the weight of it wasn't too heavy for me, I walked out of the hotel while noticing that all the other bikers were sleeping in their rooms. It was as if there really was a god and that he was looking out for me. If that was the case, then I was hoping he was going to lead me somewhere better.

I had just about enough money that he gave me to pay for a bus ride out of town. We had to go back to Los Angeles, as they said they had some unfinished business there. It didn't worry me much what it was that they were so adamant about doing there, and that was everything about it I could still remember.

For now, my focus was finding what could make me happy.

I walked over to the bus stop and stopped just below the roof of it. As the minutes passed, I realized it was unlikely any of the bikers were going to wake up and find me here. That thought comforted me, but it was still not enough to make my heart slow down.

A pair of very bright lights caught my attention as I heard the engine of the bus while it approached me. A sense of emptiness was beginning to take over me as part of me realized I missed Jim too much. He was the only one who showed me some compassion after finding out the truth about me.

The bus pulled over and I hopped on it. As soon as I was inside it, I noticed that it was empty. No one else was here with me, other than the bus driver.

I gave him the dollars that were in the pocket of my pants and sat down on one of the seats. My mind was still racing and all kinds of thoughts were popping up in it. I didn't know if I was feeling better by abandoning him, but I still couldn't imagine myself doing anything different.

After my dad showed up that time, I was still hating myself for being who I was. I was a mistake, a defect, and that was the end of it.

I didn't know where life was going to take me now, but I was hoping the destination was going to be a good one.

CHAPTER 7

Gary

After going back to Los Angeles, my only choice now was to head back to Las Vegas. The first bus I had hopped on didn't take me very far. I ended up having to get on another bus, and this one was taking me to Las Vegas. I was aware it didn't make a lot of sense I was going back there, but I still found myself with no other option. It was either this or going back to Daddy.

And even though I liked Daddy quite a lot, I couldn't imagine myself going back to him.

The bus was cruising on the street, and it was dark outside. My eyes could already see the hint of sunlight appearing in the distance, showing up just over the mountains. It was pretty and it reminded me of better times, when Paul and I were still great friends.

Smoke started to come out of the engine of the bus. I had no idea what was happening, and I was happy that, this time, I wasn't alone on the bus. It was kind of awkward last time.

The driver started to utter something to himself, which was making me feel a little worried about what was happening. The last thing I needed now was something to impede me from getting to my destination.

I tried not to think too much about that and focused on the rolling hills, small shrubs, some plants, and tumbleweeds. There was no denying that the desert was a very beautiful place. One could even say it was prettier than Las Vegas.

But the smoke that was coming out of the engine was quite thick and heavy, and it was beginning to stink. I tried covering up my nose, but it was no use. Some of the passengers on the bus started to complain about it, and we were all sharing the same opinion. Whatever was happening in the engine, we needed to pull over and get out of the bus right away.

The driver started to utter something else to himself and finally began to pull over. A mixture of relief and hatred began to overtake me, even though I didn't act on them. My mind was fully focused on getting to my destination.

When the bus screeched to a halt, a small portion of the sun was already coming up over the mountains. There weren't many mountains to speak of and they weren't very tall, but they still beautified the background.

I stepped out of the bus and sat down, waiting for the driver to figure out a solution. I didn't know if he knew a lot about fixing engines, but that would surely come in handy now.

He popped open the lid and a huge cloud of smoke billowed up against his face. He shook his arms and started to cough. I knew that thinking this was a little mean, but it was still the thought that was in my mind - at least I wasn't him now.

And now, more than ever before, I found myself wishing to be in the arms of my Daddy. I knew that he would be telling me everything was going to be okay.

Minutes passed, and it felt like this was never going to end.

I was still sitting on the pavement when the driver walked toward us. The look in his eyes was quite telling. He couldn't fix the engine by himself.

"I think I'm going to call the department. I can't fix everything on my own."

And this time, without giving it a second thought, I grabbed my paci and popped it into my mouth. I was still wearing the same diaper Jim had put on me, and it was making some volume on my hips.

All the passengers and the driver were now staring at me wide-eyed. They never suspected that one of the other passengers was just going to stand up and pop a pacifier into his mouth. They were thinking – what the hell is wrong with that guy?

The truth was a very simple one. I'd grown tired of life throwing so much shit in my direction, and now I was taking matters into my own hands. I was going to finish walking my way to Las Vegas and, from there, I'd call my friend using a pay phone.

He would be able to help me.

Minutes passed, and then they felt like hours. It was more like I was dragging myself along the road, and I didn't find it too surprising that none of the other passengers tried to stop me. After all, they all thought I was just another guy that could really... take care of himself.

At least the paci in my mouth was already making me feel better and that I could tackle all of this on my own.

Still dragging my body forward, each step feeling too heavy to take, my heart skipped a beat when I noticed that a truck was pulling over, right where I was. I didn't want to think that they might be the same person, but the resemblance couldn't be ignored.

It was the same man from before, and now he was coming for me.

I thought about ditching my backpack, but then I remembered it had all the things Daddy had bought me. All the little gifts and treats. I couldn't just get rid of them. I'd feel like complete trash.

That's why I was tightening my grip on the straps of the backpack and considering holding my ground against him. If he was thinking about kidnapping me again, then he was going to find out I wasn't the same 'damsel in distress' from before.

He pulled over, not turning off the engine while he looked at me from the top of the cabin. His eyes glared at me, and they had a sense of determination in them I'd never seen before.

I didn't know why he'd dumped me after shoving me into his truck, but I was feeling like I was soon going to find that out.

He jumped out of the truck, marching toward me like his body was growing and he was becoming more like a huge lion. He latched his hand around my wrist and started to drag me toward the truck.

I tried fighting back, snapping my head from side to side, but I couldn't see anyone. As if to continue mocking me further, the road was deserted. No cars and trucks were driving in this direction, and it was like the whole thing had been set up for this to be happening.

"Let go of me, you brute! I don't have anything to do with you!" My throat was dry. I hadn't drunk anything in hours.

"No, you're coming with me," he affirmed, spilling saliva out of his mouth. I felt like punching him right now. If only I had the strength to do that, I'd be doing so right now.

He threw open the door of the truck and shoved me inside it. I tried kicking him, but he was again latching his hands around my ankles and stopping me. I really didn't know what he was thinking he was doing, but my heart was speeding up and I was feeling I would never see the light of day again.

He reached around somewhere in the back with his hand, picking up something. I was still thrashing my body about so much I couldn't quite focus on what it was that he was now holding in his hand.

I felt it being put around my ankles much before I had any time to react. It was duct tape, which he was now also gluing on my mouth.

"You fucking piece of shit. I really do prefer it when you don't fight back. Next time, I'm going to bring the syringe," he mentioned, and I guessed I should consider myself lucky that he hadn't done that. I didn't know what I'd be doing now if he was drugging me.

I couldn't move anymore. He'd finished putting the duct tape on my ankles and wrists, and I was sweating and surprised I managed to fight back that much. I thought I didn't have the strength anymore to pull something like that off.

He wiped the sweat off his forehead, relaxing in his seat and looking at the road in front of him. I didn't know what was going on in his mind, but I wasn't about to ask.

"I hope he's going to pay me well," he said, and I couldn't help but wonder who he was referring to.

I couldn't talk, but it wasn't like he couldn't read my mind, either.

"You don't worry, boy. I'm going to take you back to your father."

And it was then that all of this was making sense to me. Dad was also a trucker, and he was quite good at his job. So good that he knew all sorts of people. It wasn't too far-fetched that he knew this man and I didn't. After all, I didn't like meeting his friends.

Still trying not to have a panic attack, I let my head drop on the door and felt the rumbling of the engine as he turned it on. He pulled at the gear stick and then shoved it forward, stepping on the accelerator.

I couldn't hope to stop him. The only way of stopping him now was by... hoping my Daddy or one of the other bikers would soon find out about my disappearance. But it was unlikely either of those things was going to happen, given the small number of people who knew about what I was doing.

I should have, at least, given them a hint about where I was heading to.

Minutes passed, and then it felt like they were more like hours. He was taking me out of the desert, heading North in the state of California. I didn't know where he thought he was taking me to, but his behavior was all kinds of weird. Shouldn't he be taking me to Los Angeles, where my father should be sleeping at this time of the night?

I didn't know, and I couldn't say anything right now. The duct tape couldn't be moved, ripped off, and I couldn't even move my arms. I tried to scream, but the sound was coming out muffled. Not to mention that, thanks to the constant rumbling of the engine, I couldn't be heard anyway, even though we were already seeing some cars and motorcycles again.

Motorcycles... None of them looked like Harley-Davidsons or Hondas, I noticed.

The trucker wasn't even talking to me, but the fact that he was driving me to the North of California, where San Francisco was, showed me that my father was working there. He was 'living' somewhere there now.

Minutes later, I was seeing San Francisco in the distance when he turned right. What the hell? I snapped my head toward him and thought that, for sure, something was deeply wrong. But he was still not looking at me, focused on his destination instead.

I couldn't hope to understand what was going on in his mind, though his smirk was exuding his overconfidence. Of course he was going to be like that, after manhandling me and shoving me into his truck with so little effort. If I'd thought before that I could have fought back, I'd been a fool.

Trees appeared behind the small hill we were on, and I had no idea what he thought he was doing. He couldn't just be taking me to my father. He was taking me into a forest, and over there the police were going to have a hard time finding me.

I just wanted to be held by Jim again.

CHAPTER 8

Jim

Opening my eyes, the first thing I did was to put my arm around him. Keeping him protected all the time was paramount to me, and right now, nothing was wrong between us. I was in love with him, and I was pretty sure he was thinking the same thing, too. I couldn't wait until I was putting another diaper on him. He was going to wake up this morning finding it soiled, as usual. His continence shamed him a little, even though I already told him several times he didn't need to feel that way about it.

A sense of emptiness overtook me. Rays of light were shining through the blinds. Sleeping in a hotel room had its perks, though there was still nothing like sleeping with your mates in tents outside of town.

I was still in Las Vegas. A little close to The Strip, but not too much so. I could have paid for a room in one of the casino hotels, but I didn't want to be in a place that was so dirty and noisy all the time. I hadn't made that decision for myself, but for my little one.

My little one... I couldn't feel him at all, and that made my heart go from normal to racing in seconds.

I sat up on the bed with the speed of a lightning bolt, snapping my head from side to side, only to find out that the worst thing was happening. My little one had walked out on me in the middle of the night, and now I didn't have any idea where he could be.

A thought crossed my mind. It could be possible that the police had ended up tracking him down and taken him back to his father. I couldn't imagine what he might be feeling now, if that was the case. Lost, desperate, and begging for me to come to find him.

I shot off the bed, trying to put on my clothes and almost falling over. I wasn't in my right state of mind, and it showed. In fact, my mind was racing so much that my heart was feeling tight, and I was feeling I was soon going to have a heart attack.

I managed to finish putting on my pants and shirt, but just barely. I snagged my leather jacket from the garment rack and threw it on me. I was rushing out of the room before I could plan out what I should be doing right now. All I was thinking was that I needed to find my little one right away, and damned be the consequences.

I wanted to hold him in my arms and tell him that everything was going to be alright. Was that too much to ask?

Not thinking about that much, I stormed into the main hallway. Terry and Ramon were discussing something, throwing their arms about. I was no mind reader, but it was more than evident that they also already knew about Gary's disappearance.

"We need to do something! We need to call him." He didn't mention his name, but I was pretty sure he was still referring to the contact we now had in the police in Las Vegas. He was one of the main reasons why we were managing to dodge the authorities so far.

They snapped their heads in my direction, widening their eyes when they noticed it was me.

"Jim, you must have already heard about it. One of the guys noticed he was going to one of the bus stops, but he hasn't seen him since. He thought Gary was just going out for a snack or something like that."

My heart was tight, but I was still going to remain calm.

"I know about what happened, and I agree with Ramon. We need to call our friend and tell him what happened. It's the only way we're going to get out of this mess and find him.

Their discussion wasn't if they should call Larry or not, but that they were worried about the possible consequences of doing that. We never resorted to asking for favors like that unless it was an emergency, and right now, it was. Terry might not have fully accepted that yet, but since he also had a little and he knew how important he was to him, he didn't have another choice.

He nodded and whirled around on his ankles. He was going to do the right thing, despite the possible consequences.

He pulled out his phone and dialed a sequence of numbers. My palms were beginning to grow sweaty, and the only thing I was still worried about was if Gary was okay. My little was the most important person in the world to me.

I crossed my arms and was tapping with my foot on the floor while I waited for him to finish the call. I couldn't make out everything that he was saying, but I trusted him and so did everyone else in the club.

He ended the call and then turned around to face me again. His eyes were fierce, but he was looking at me with hope. I was waiting for him to give me the location and then, as soon as I knew where my little might be, I would raise hell to find him.

"He wants to meet us in person. Outside the city, where he thinks it's the only safe place."

"I know," I affirmed with determination, rushing out of the hotel. I didn't need to worry about paying for the room, since it was already paid for.

I hopped on my bike and took up after Terry told me where the destination was. My hands were sweatier than ever before and despite all the complications I went through in my life, part of me was feeling like this was the worst of them.

It took me almost no time to reach the spot where that guy had set up for the meeting. It was outside the city, and from here we had the perfect view of it. We could see all the main buildings, and it was already a relief that I wasn't there anymore.

It wasn't a police car that showed up, but a guy on a bike. He didn't have any patches on his leather jacket, but it was still pretty evident that he wished he was more like us. After all, that pair of aviator sunglasses and leather jacket couldn't hide the truth.

Some time had already passed since we made the call. All the money he needed from us, we already had it in our suitcases. We were going to give them to him, and he would ride out of here a much richer man. And, perhaps he could even end up using that money to leave the police for good.

I hoped that wasn't the case. His information had been reliable and vital so far.

"I think we know where he might be. We've been tracking everyone coming in and out of the hotel. We couldn't act based on suspicions alone, but a young guy about Gary's age walked out of the building and is heading north, toward San Francisco."

San Francisco? My heart skipped a beat and even though I was sitting on my Guardian, I was still tapping on the ground with my foot. I couldn't hide how nervous I was about this whole thing.

"You've been keeping tabs on us?" That was Ramon speaking. I didn't know why he was acting so surprised. It was more than evident that the police were still maintaining their investigation on us.

Larry nodded, shifting his eyes down towards the suitcases. He wasn't going to say anything else until he got his money.

I was holding one of the suitcases. I might not be in my right state of mind, but I was the treasurer of the club, and all the money in it went through me.

"Here's some of it. Now tell us the rest. We need an exact location," I affirmed, missing the beating of Gary's heart. That was just one of the things about him I needed right now, though I couldn't also hide how much I wanted to change his diaper again.

I could only wonder how he was feeling right now, without someone to do that for him.

After saying that, I tossed the suitcase I was holding towards him. It skidded over the ground and stopped by his feet. Seeing that, he picked it up.

"Fine. He's taking him here, and his name is Aubrey. We don't know all the details, but it kind of looks like he will take him back to his father. You need to get there as soon as possible. We're going to storm the place and jail that greasy trucker. We've been looking for excuses to cuff him for a very long time, and now he's finally making a mistake."

I didn't find that too surprising, but it was still making my hands sweatier. The last thing I needed was to have to work my way through a police blockade.

"I'm going there," I told everyone in the club and they weren't surprised. They knew I couldn't wait much longer, and each passing second was crucial.

I twisted the throttle of the bike and took off. Going from here to San Francisco was going to take a long time. Part of me was asking if it wouldn't be possible to take a plane instead, but I didn't even have a passport.

Wind, heat, dehydration, and the fact I missed Gary too much almost made me think I was going to pass out. It was thanks to my determination, more than anything, that that didn't come to pass.

Larry had given us an exact location, and we only needed to find it. Thanks to GPS and our phones, that proved to be an easier process than I'd thought.

I was standing now in the middle of a room in a building made of wood planks. The interior was dark, but sure enough, my little was there.

He was sitting on a chair and cuffed to it. I wouldn't be feeling okay even if that was everything Aubrey had done to him. He'd also put duct tape on his ankles and wrists, and that was making my blood boil.

This was inhumane in all levels possible, and it was making me want to punch the guy until blood was coming out.

"Thought I was going to find you here," a man said from within the shadows in the barn. I wasn't alone. All the citizens of the club were here with me, and we had guns this time.

If it came to it, I wouldn't be opposed to using them.

My eyes shifted to Gary. His eyelids were closed and his head was lolled to one side. I didn't think he'd been harmed so much that he'd passed out, but if that was the case, I wouldn't object to punching the shit out of his father.

He was the one standing now in front of Gary, lifting his arms as if he was taunting me to hurt him.

The only reason why I wasn't doing such a thing was that I knew the police were coming soon and that they would put him behind bars as well.

All the other bikers also were here and they provided the backup I needed. Not that I thought I couldn't beat him in a fair fight, but that I preferred if things didn't come to that.

"You think that this will pan out the way you're hoping?" He said before lunging at me.

He wasn't giving me any choice. I didn't want to hurt him because I feared what my little would think of this, but I was still not going to hold anything back.

I punched him straight in his face. His eyes were red and his breath stank of alcohol. I didn't know his full story and it didn't matter to me at all, but it was more than clear he'd been drinking a lot before he did what he did.

Sirens started to echo in the distance, and after his body fell as a cloud of soil billowed up, I knew this was over before it started.

Shifting my eyes upward, I rushed to my little and pulled out a small knife from one of the pockets of my pants.

I started to cut the duct tape, and then put him in my arms. Tears were rolling down my cheeks and the only thing I was thinking about now was taking him to a hospital. It needed to be a good one, too.

My little could have only the best.

CHAPTER 9

Jim

He was opening his eyes and looking at me. This was like our first meeting, but even better than that. He was turning his head and looking at me with wondering eyes. He was asking himself if he could remember what happened, and I wasn't going to be making any questions about that to him.

I moved my hand and grabbed his. My grip was firm and warm. He was pressing his fingers back against my hand and allowing his eyes to look more comfortable.

As long as my little was with me, everything would be fine. That's what he was thinking right now.

When I found him in that cabin in the woods, he didn't have his diaper on anymore. I didn't know what had happened, but only one possibility was coming to my mind.

His father, during his moment of craziness and reverie, took his diaper off him and tossed it somewhere. That bore no importance to me as it still didn't mean he was hurt.

In fact, Gary was looking so dirty and had passed out thanks to his own actions. He shouldn't have walked out of the hotel and tried to go back on his own to Las Vegas. He couldn't live without someone to love him at all times.

All I knew was that I was more than overjoyed I was with him again. We had rented another room for a couple of nights, and I wasn't feeling bad about that at all. In fact, I'd be renting a proper, more permanent flat for us after everything that happened if I had the money.

He retreated his hand and put it on his belly. He was now looking at the ceiling and saying, "I'm sorry about everything that happened. I shouldn't have walked out like that. It was stupid, and I feel stupid."

"Hey, it's okay. You don't need to feel so bad about it. It was a one-time thing and I'm pretty sure everything is going to be much better now."

"You're right about that," he said, his cheeks looking so kissable right now.

After a moment passed, I looped my fingers around the plastic strap and pulled up a small bag.

Gary turned his eyes until he was looking at it. I thought he needed something to perk him up after he woke up, and this was perfect for that.

"Oh, you didn't do that," he said, and there was no reason to skirt around it. I'd been planning on doing this with him for a long time, and I was so happy it was finally being realized.

"But I did," I said with a happy smile on my face while opening the small bag and taking a mask out of it. It looked like a puppy, and it was already bringing a smile to his tired face.

That tiredness on his face... I was going to do something about it. I was going to heal him.

I took one other thing out of the small bag. A pair of mittens. He was going to love putting them on.

"Oh, they look so lovely!" He said in happiness, already shifting until he was sitting up better.

I ruffled his hair with my hand and fished something else out of the small bag, which widened his smile. A pair of paws so that he could crawl and run around with a tail on, which was also in the small bag.

He'd mentioned so many times he would love to play like a puppy with me, and me being me, I couldn't help but realize that dream for him.

Other than those things, I also bought him a pair of dog ears. They looked a little heavy and they were certainly going to look big on him, but I was still pretty sure he was going to put them on with a smile on his face.

He was resting in the hotel's bed, but I was pretty sure he could get off it and play with me. Considering the twinkling in his eyes, it was more than evident that's what he wanted to do now.

I put all the puppy play things on a small table and then held out my hand. He moved his hand and grabbed mine. His hand felt soft and very sweet, and I was so overjoyed with all this I couldn't hide my smile.

I took him off the bed and admired his body from bottom to top. To me, the most important thing was knowing that it didn't matter what happened from now on, but that he was always going to be here. I was going to make sure of that.

"Well, I think I need to start by undressing you."

I put my fingers underneath his shirt. Before we brought him to the room, I bought him some new clothes. The ones he had weren't good enough for him. He was the most special person to me, and he should only have the best.

I lifted the shirt and took it off him. His chest looked skinny and small, and I loved it.

Not thinking about anything in particular now, I put the shirt down on the small table and then took off his pants.

He didn't have a diaper on, though I was soon going to fix that. I couldn't let my little walk around without it, after all.

Having taken off his pants, I realized he didn't have any underwear on, too. I didn't know what was going on in his father's mind at the time, but it was more than obvious that he needed to be put in a psychiatric hospital.

I tried not letting those things ruin the moment, focusing on taking him to the bathroom. I was leading him there by putting my hand on his back, and he was obeying me with a huge smile on his face.

After taking him there, I ripped open a small package and dumped in the water the powder that was inside of it. After getting on my knees and shaking my right hand in the water, bubbles started to show up.

I stood up again and said, "That's right, little one. You're going to get a bubble bath tonight as well."

He widened his smile and was already putting his right foot in the water until I stopped him. I shook my finger in front of his eyes.

"Not right now. We're still missing an important piece of the puzzle."

Hearing that, he lifted one of his eyebrows.

It was a small, yellow plastic duck. The red beak made it look a little funny. I picked it up and gave it to him. His eyes contemplated it in wonder, and he looked so cute I couldn't help but feel like kissing him.

"Now, you can finally get in the water," I said, and he was already putting one of his feet in it. Then, he dropped his body in it, splashing water all over. I put my hands on my waist and looked at him with judging eyes. He shouldn't have done that, but it was okay. I didn't care that my clothes got wet.

I bathed him with a bath soap bar that smelled of magnolia. I loved sliding the sponge on his body, feeling every curve of it, and the happy gleaming in his eyes, as I did that, was unmistakable. He loved this just as much as I did.

After bathing him, I took him out of the bathtub and then toweled him dry. He was a little and needed me to do everything for him, which was great. I loved that part about being his caregiver.

His hair was a little messy, and I combed it after his body was dry. His pee-pee had gotten hard, but I decided not to play with it right now. He'd already lost his virginity to me before, and now he could focus on enjoying this moment with me.

I took him back to the bedroom and laid him down in the bed. As soon as I was done with that, I took out a bottle of talcum and soothing cream for his butt. After spreading them on him, just like that other time, I put a new diaper on him.

I was cherishing every second of this and loving the fact I was more proficient at changing his diaper.

But that wasn't the end of our puppy roleplay. I picked up the paws I'd shown him before, put them on him, and proceeded to put the small tiara with ears on his head. He already looked so cute with those on, and I hadn't even finished dressing him as a pup yet.

I grabbed a small belt that had the tail. After snapping the front of it, he started to wag his butt, as if he were a real pup. He even started to arf and hold his hands in front of him as if he was asking for a treat.

I slapped his butt gently and then picked up the mittens. After putting them on him, I settled my hands on my waist and admired him for a moment. He looked so sweet I wanted to be holding him with all of my strength right now.

It was also so great that his transformation hadn't even finished yet.

I grabbed a collar and snapped it around his neck. He looked more than cute with it now, especially with the leash the collar had. When I grabbed it, he was already falling to his knees while putting his hands on the floor.

He started to arf with his mouth and wag his tail. I loved everything about him, and was chuckling and laughing with him while taking him around the apartment for a stroll. He continued to bark and the smile on his face couldn't hide the happiness that was overflowing from his heart, but this was still far from everything that we were going to do together tonight.

We didn't feel okay with doing any of this outside, so this was the only spot we had. As soon as this was over, we were going to buy a house and settle down, just like Ramon and Lucas were considering doing. I sure as hell was hoping they were going to be successful in their venture.

After playing around with him and taking a stroll in the apartment, which was small, I grabbed a small plastic toy from that same bag, which had all the other items. Gary was already sitting on his knees and arfing again, putting his tongue out and breathing through his mouth.

I looked at that and chuckled. This was the first time he was roleplaying as a pup, and he was already looking all sorts of cute.

I threw the bone gently and it bounced off a wall as pup Gary rushed towards it. It occurred to me that I should choose a pup name for him one day, but that was a thing for another time and place.

After he picked it up with his mouth, he made two circles and started to gnaw on it instead of taking it to me right away. I looked at that and chuckled again, shuffling over to him and ruffling his hair.

I kissed his cheek and then swung my arms around him, hugging and falling over with him on the floor. I couldn't hide the happiness inside of me, and it was showing in the huge smile on my face.

If it were possible, I'd be reliving this moment all of my life.

GARY'S EPILOGUE

I never thought he'd be taking me here. The prison, where they were keeping my dad. He was the one behind the whole thing. The trucker was also here, in one of their cells and awaiting final judgment.

My hands were sweaty. I was looking from side to side, standing outside the prison. It was located on the outskirts of San Francisco, and the surrounding area was a sight to behold. Mountains after mountains, hills, and more and more desert. I felt like I was in some kind of dream put in a nightmare.

The waves of anxiety that were rolling through my body couldn't be ignored. Jim was holding my hand, but even that wasn't enough to quench it. All I knew was that I wasn't going to walk out of this as the same person. It was going to change everything I knew about myself, and I didn't know if that was a good or a bad thing.

Not thinking much more about that, I felt Jim's hand squeezing mine a little more tightly. It was his signal to make me look up at him. He was so much taller than me that I always had to look up at him, even when we were sitting.

We walked over into the building and went through the lobby. My father had requested to meet up with me, and I didn't know why. Part of me was saying that he felt bad about everything he did, but I couldn't be sure about that without seeing him again.

We walked down a corridor and were soon finding ourselves in the room where he was going to meet us. My heart skipped a beat when I realized that the booth, on the other side, was empty. I couldn't see my father anywhere, and that was making my hands sweatier.

I sat down and Jim rested his body on a wall, putting one of his hands on my right shoulder. He was comforting me, and I couldn't be doing this without him.

The door on the other side, after the transparent panel, opened and in stepped my father. He had typical orange garments on and looked so much worse than his usual self. I shouldn't be feeling sorry for him and, yet, I still was.

One of the prison guards was accompanying him. He led my father to me and advised him 'not to try anything funny.' I thought I knew my father. Before now, I'd be saying with certainty that he would never do anything crazy, but I knew better this time.

Had I really disappointed him so much that he was willing to do what he did, going through so much just to make me feel I was wrong?

He sighed and said, "I suppose I should be saying I was wrong about you all this time."

What? I couldn't believe what he was saying to me right now. He was telling me that he felt sorry for having treated me like trash?

Jim huffed. "You're not trying to make me believe you're going to try to make up for everything you did, right?"

"I don't think it will come to that, but I'm trying to become someone better. What I did can't be forgiven, and I see that now."

"After you were put in jail," Jim accused, still keeping his arms crossed. Meanwhile, I was keeping my hands between my legs, my posture hunched as I found it difficult to figure out what I should be thinking about this.

I never thought that, all of a sudden, he would be telling me that he was feeling sorry.

"That's right, after that."

"I'm not ready to forgive you yet," I said, straightening up my spine and ascertaining myself that I was doing the right thing. The most important thing now was hearing his other side of what he did.

"That's alright, you shouldn't be doing that. I tried turning you into a person that couldn't exist, and I'm really sorry for that."

Jim huffed again, and he looked like he couldn't believe a word of what my father was saying. I shared some of his thoughts, though being Paul's son was making me feel more prone to give him… another chance, perhaps?

I didn't know if I could say that. All I knew was that this was a mess, and that the room we were in was getting hotter by the second.

Father turned his eyes until he was looking at me again.

"You're not going to say anything else, my son? You should come to visit me here again."

Visiting him again wasn't something I thought I was ready for. Not yet. This moment was good for gauging what he was like now, but I didn't feel like coming here another time yet.

He sighed and stood up.

"I'm really sorry about everything that happened, and when I'm out of here, I won't look for you," he promised.

His eyes did have a mixture of something I couldn't quite… put my finger on. Maybe he'd lost hope or something like that. Either way, he was already turning around and leaving. The door on the other side of the room closed, and I knew I wouldn't be seeing him in a pretty long time.

My Daddy squeezed my shoulder a little harder, and he grabbed my hand while we stood up. I was happy that part of me was settled for now, though nothing could ever change what Paul had put me through. All the tears would never dry.

We walked out of the prison and were soon seated on the Guardian. Jim didn't turn on the engine yet, but put his arms around me, letting me rest my head on his chest. It was one of the few things about this that were comforting me, and I would never be doing this without him.

The warmth of his body was like nothing else I'd felt. Well, I'd bathed myself in it many other times, but there was still something special about this moment.

I guessed that was due to all the emotional overload that was coming out of my meeting with Paul.

He was putting one of his hands on my cheek, caressing it, and turning my head until I was looking at him.

"It doesn't matter all the things he said to you. I'm not sure if he was lying, but I still don't trust him. You're your own person now, and you've got me as well."

"It's up to me now if I can forgive him or not," I admitted and hugged Jim more tightly. There was one thing I was looking forward to right now, and that was going back home.

We'd finally decided to settle down in our own place. It was a two-bedroom flat close to downtown San Diego. We were still going to live in California and continue to enjoy all the good things it provided to us. And, in turn, we were also going to have all the privacy to do the things we wanted.

I couldn't wait until I was a puppy again. We did it that time, but there were still so many things about it we hadn't explored yet.

"That's right, little one, and I'm sure you're going to make the right decision," he said, pushing me gently until I was getting off the bike. But he was only doing that because he wanted me to sit on the back of it and to put my arms around him again.

He twisted the throttle after opening an easy smile on his face. Daddy was always so confident, and that was showing right now.

The rumbling of the engine of the Guardian tuned out everything around me, allowing me to focus just on the man of my life.

He fished out something from the pocket of his pants. It was a pacifier. One of mine, and I was already opening my mouth and waiting for it to come in.

With the pacifier positioned between my lips, it was seven easier for me not to have to worry about anything.

He twisted the throttle again, getting some judgmental looks from the prison guards, and then he took off like the only goal in his life now was getting to where the sun was setting.

There was nothing like riding on the Guardian.

JIM'S EPILOGUE

We couldn't be doing this without entering his little space again. But his little headspace was somewhat different than most of the others. He was already getting himself in the mood, putting himself on his knees, and settling his hands on the floor.

Our new apartment was small, but we weren't thinking about adding anyone else to the family. Now that Terry was the only one from the old guard still riding with the club, I was pretty sure he was feeling like a new chapter was beginning in his life.

I felt a little bad that we were leaving him alone, though. I was hoping that soon we would get more people to join the club.

I put the small tiara with the ears on his head, and he arfed and stuck his tongue out. I was going to do all the other things I did with him that other time, and also some other things I'd been planning on doing with him.

I couldn't wait until his transformation was finished again.

He had his diaper on, and it was smelling just like him.

After putting that cute tiara on him, I proceeded to slide the mittens on his hands. With his paws on, he looked even cuter than ever, and I couldn't help but rub his belly.

He didn't say anything, but he did arf again and showed me that he was loving every minute of this. The bright, big smile on his face couldn't be mistaken for anything else, after all.

After tickling his belly and also his armpits, I proceeded to put the paws on his feet before he could recompose himself. When he reopened his googly eyes, he was staring at them wide-eyed, and looking more than surprised that he already had them on.

That still didn't mean his transformation was already finished, of course. I picked up the belt with the tail, put it on him, and snapped the front. He looked so docile I was pretty sure he couldn't hurt a fly, even if he was trying to do that.

With the tail, his transformation was already finished. Gary was, in seconds, lying on his back, which meant I was also already putting my hand on his belly. I was teasing him that I was going to tickle him again, and he had a dirty smile on his face.

But that smile was hidden by his paci. The front of it was shaped like a bone, which fit his new self to perfection.

"You're loving every second of this, aren't you?" I asked, widening the smile on my face which couldn't be hidden.

His skin was smooth and soft, and I was moving one of my fingers in circles. His weak spot when it came to tickling was his belly button. His skin was also white and very peachy. His cheeks bore a tone of blush that he couldn't get rid of. It never mattered what he was or wasn't doing. He was always blushing.

I started to rub my hand on his belly without warning him, loving how he was kicking the air and trying to make me stop with his hands. Those things didn't represent the reality in his mind, that he wanted me to continue that, and knowing his wishes, I couldn't help but rub his tummy several more times.

The pacifier in his mouth even came off, but I picked it up before he realized that, and put it in his mouth again.

After I stopped tickling him, he returned to normal and his breathing slowed down. Belly rubbing him wasn't going to be enough, though I was keeping some other things for later.

I stood up and he got back on his knees, already crawling around without using them for that. He, in fact, was keeping his body in a familiar, bent shape as he did that and started to make circles around me.

The whole time, he was barking and pretending that he was breathing through his mouth, just like a real pup would.

One good thing about living in this flat, even though it was small, was that the soundproofing was top-notch. It was so good that little Gary didn't have to worry about the level of noise he was making.

After he finished crawling around me and his breathing quickened, I grabbed his leash and started to lead him through the flat. With no more than a couple of rooms to explore, he couldn't have the experience I was hoping I could provide for him, and that was okay.

We did have a balcony, though, even if it was also somewhat small and we didn't have space for everything we wanted in it. I sat down and scooped him up from the floor, putting little Gary on my lap.

He cradled himself until he was in a comfortable position. My dick was getting hard, and I wouldn't be surprised if tonight ended with me fucking his bubble butt. It was so lovely and it made me think about it all the time.

Gary purred and shifted a little more, until he was finding the right position that made him feel comfortable. I put my hand on his head and started to move it over it gently, taking in the view of the setting sun in the distance. The sky's color was changing to a hue of orange, gold, and red, and it was calming as much as it was pretty.

I didn't have my phone right now with me, but I'd be taking a selfie with him otherwise. And, if I also had his permission, I'd be posting that photo online with a caption. It would be saying something along the lines of, 'this is how we are like and nothing and no one will ever be able to change that.'

Minutes later, he pushed himself off my lap and started to run to the bedroom. My legs were like they were made of bricks, but I still jumped off the chair and started to chase after him. If he was thinking he was going to manage to run away from me, then he had something coming!

I was storming through the doorway to the bedroom, finding him lying in the bed. He had his tail between his legs and was still breathing with his tongue out of his mouth.

I jumped into the bed and put my arms around him. His body

was as warm as before and he was giggling so much he almost started to cough. When I put my finger on his lips, he calmed down a little and shifted until he was better cradled in the comfort of my arms.

I moved my hand up and took off his tiara. He didn't need to keep pretending that he was a little doggie anymore if he didn't feel like it.

He took a deep breath and shifted until he was sealing his lips with mine. They were so sweet, and I couldn't help but slide my tongue through them. Gary, being the little that he was and who couldn't live without me, soon started to moan.

My dick was harder than it had ever been, and I knew that tonight was going to end with him giving himself to me again.

It couldn't be happening any other way.

The End

Did you know? You can now just rate books on Amazon, instead of having to write full reviews! Just click on how many stars you want to give it and that's it. If you liked this story and could do that, you'd be helping us a lot. Thank you for reading it!

MORE MM ABDL? YES!

My Loving Biker: An ABDL MM Biker Romance (Sweet Pacis #2)

Lucas

Oh man, this job sucked so bad. I couldn't wrap my head around it. I should be studying in a college. Living in Los Angeles and, especially, in California, I had some pretty good options. There was UC at Los Angeles and Stanford. I didn't know what I was still doing here, working at Burger King...

Was I thinking that I had a future working there?

Of course not, but I still lived with my parents. I know, I know. I was 19 and I should have already gotten out of the nest. It was more difficult for me to do so than it was for other people.

I didn't have any problems with making friends. I actually had a lot of them and, even now, while I was walking across this sidewalk and pretending that this part of the city wasn't scary, they were already flooding my phone with messages and audios.

It was a mess, and I was reserving this time now to think a little about my life. After everything that happened today at my job, I was thinking I needed a little of me time. Sometimes, that helped a lot to make me feel better.

The wind was whirling around me and I didn't know why. I was usually so busy that I didn't bother to check the weather. I supposed that it was going to rain tonight and we were going to have a raging thunderstorm.

Didn't even want to think about that, considering the history of thunderstorms in this region. More often than not, they knocked down trees, which in turn snapped the powerlines.

Well, if that happened, I was already making a promise to myself. I'd pick up my phone and invite all of my friends. We would party and I'd have the time of my life, all the while pretending that I was just like them.

I was just kidding.

I wasn't anything like them.

They didn't know about a little secret of mine. When they weren't looking or around, I put a pacifier in my mouth and a diaper around my hips. I loved becoming a little and pretending that I was a kid all over again.

I couldn't help but be nostalgic, after all. Was there a better moment in a person's life that wasn't their childhood? I couldn't think so. I always thought that their golden years happened when they didn't have to worry about anything.

Point being, becoming an adult sucked, and having a job sucked even more. Not to mention that I was seeing all of my friends going to college, building their lives while here I was, stuck again at that 9-8 job. I always had to work extra time to make ends meet.

Out here in Los Angeles, the minimum wage was pretty much useless. I couldn't remember when it was the last time I felt like I could buy anything substantial with it. More often than not, that money was used to pay the bills and buy food at the local Walmart.

I turned to the right, already noticing the change in the scenery around me. Gone were the tall buildings and in were the small houses with almost no space between them. I didn't know how people could live like that.

I mean, I kind of knew. We lived in a pretty similar house, and it was so close to the others it was almost like we were living all together in one big place. I could hear them sneezing, when they argued, shouting, and even peeing.

I needed a new place, and badly.

Now, it wouldn't be too bad if I could move around the country freely. That's one thing I envied the most about bikers. They didn't have to live in just one place. They could go from one spot to the other, and they didn't even have to pay property tax. How cool was that?

That's one other thing I was sure would never happen in my life, alongside finding a boyfriend that understood me. I could have a fling here and there with a guy, but finding one that was a Daddy?

Now, that was impossible.

Not to mention that they all thought the terminology used was weird. Daddies, littles, pacifiers, and whatnot. Lonely struck me every night, sometimes leading to insomnia.

I ignored the lack of street lamps in this street. Not too long now until I got home. It was just a thirty-minute walk and whenever I was thinking about life as much as I was thinking now, then it was usually much shorter. Or just felt it was. I knew space couldn't be shortened like that.

That's why I was hoping everything was going to be okay. No weirdos showing up, no beggars, and especially no criminals thinking that I had anything worthwhile. I mean, I did have my phone with me, but it had been like 200 dollars when I bought it, and that was a couple of years ago.

I turned to the left, shifting my eyes left and right because I knew I was entering a more dangerous part of the city. It wasn't Skid Row, but if one wasn't careful around here, they could get mugged with ease.

I breathed a sigh of relief.

Thankfully, it appeared that there were no criminals around.

Did I ever feel like I could tell my parents about my little side? Probably not. It probably would never happen because I was still too dependent on them, and they were very religious. Like, religious to the point of putting up Christian totems in the house and saying things like how much they hated gay people.

And that the new president was gay because he didn't have a firm stance on them.

I had to do everything hidden from my father, especially when he and mom weren't around and I could play as a little for a while. I usually put on a different diaper then, grabbed my hidden collections of pacis and pretended that Snowball could speak with me.

He was my Teddy Bear. He looked old and pretty worn out, with some holes in him and cuts, but he was still the only friend that I truly trusted with everything that was happening in my life.

Ramon

I never thought they would merge so well together. They were living such a happy life now, though Carson still had some things to figure out with their parents. They couldn't wrap their heads around it. And I could understand where they were coming from.

At least it seemed they were figuring things out. As for me, I was trying to get there, too. Terry knew I was gay, and I was surprised when they told me about the little/Daddy thing.

Since then, I'd been putting a lot of effort into learning more about it. I hadn't known anything about it previously. When they talked about it for the first time and when I saw Carson with a onesie on, I worried that they were going mad or something like that.

But no, it wasn't anything like that. The truth behind it was wholly different. They were only doing what completed them. Terry now always had a big smile on his face, and Carson was always cracking jokes and smiling from ear to ear, too.

Seeing them now lying in their tent and cuddling each other, I couldn't help but find myself wondering when love would happen to me again. I'd loved once.

A guy I thought I knew. I really, really thought that he was the one I'd been looking for my whole life, but then he showed me that he'd been nothing more than a snitch.

He was a traitor. He smooth-talked his way into the club, making us all believe that he was one of ours, and then he showed us his true colors. It almost destroyed everything we'd built. Terry and the rest of the gang had to flee, and even now we were still worried that the FBI was going to lock us up.

I was lying in my tent, swiping left or right on Tinder. There were plenty of good-looking guys in the region and I was getting a few matches, too. They were all sending messages saying they wanted to meet me in person.

I couldn't help but smile. A lingering thought in my mind kept nagging me about my age, though. I mean, I was over thirty but that didn't mean I looked old.

Not to mention that most of the guys that were matching with me were younger, too. In their early twenties, with cute baby faces I loved. I had a thing for that, and I wasn't going to deny it.

The night was serene, with only a few crickets chirping outside. We could see Los Angeles and it wasn't too far from us. It didn't have much of a skyline, but it still looked pretty, like in the movies.

Now, when you actually go into the city, that's a different matter altogether. Rising poverty, beggars, and most people would say that even we were a part of that problem, too.

I was getting a little bored, though. Tinder was fine for the first few minutes, but then I realized that most of the conversations there were pretty shallow.

Like the ones I was having now.

But then, I met a guy. He had blond hair, a lean body and was cute, and with pretty, rosy cheeks that caught my attention. We started to chat and I didn't think it was going to lead to anything worthwhile, but after a few hours merging well with him, I couldn't deny that I was already thinking about going to see him.

I lifted my head from the phone and looked outside. The tent in front of me, which belonged to Carson and Terry, was now closed. I opened a shy smile while I thought how good it would be if I could have that same kind of experience again in my life.

But first, I'd start with something small. The last thing I wanted was to fall into another trap. What if I came across another snitch looking to bring down the Spectral Rats again?

I would never be able to forgive myself if that happened. I was doing this for myself, sure, but I wasn't selfish enough to put the well-being of my family at risk.

Not to mention that I didn't have another family and I didn't think I'd ever find another, safe for finding the second love of my life.

I stood up after getting that guy's address. It looked like he was in one of the less safe parts of the city. Without thinking twice about it, I picked up my Glock and put it in my waist. I wasn't going to take any chances.

I didn't have a license for concealed carry, but it wasn't like we were thinking about staying here for long. It was more likely that we would be leaving Los Angeles before we knew it was happening.

As bikers, we didn't have a permanent home, even if the thought of having one, one day, excited me. I wondered what that would be like. Living in just one place, buying things to make it better, and sharing every night with my loved one in the same bed...

Just the thought of doing that one day made me open a smile.

It was with that thought in mind that I walked out of the tent, glanced at Terry's tent, and then headed to my Harley. I named it Courage and it was a model Harley Davidson Iron 883, which wasn't the most luxurious they had, but it worked well for me.

I got on my Harley and started her up. The roar of the engine was like music to my ears and, for a moment, I just listened to it, not thinking about anything in particular.

I took off after remembering the cute face of the guy I was going to meet. I wanted to be touching him, to kiss him, and to think that love was possible again for me.

I entered the city and traversed through the wide roads, getting nearer to my goal. He should be not too far from here, and he said that he was going to meet me in a bar.

It was supposed to be a very gay-friendly place and, from the photos I'd seen of it, it was also pretty cozy.

BOOKS IN THIS SERIES

My Loving Biker: An ABDL MM Biker Romance
My Caring Biker: An ABDL MM Biker Romance

MORE LIKE THIS

Regressing the Rookie: A Gay Age Play Romance
Regressing the Recruit: An ABDL Romance
Be my ABDL: A Gay Age Play Romance
Cute Diapers Bundle: 3 Gay ABDL Romance Stories
Loving Little Chris: An ABDL MM Romance
Sugar Mister: An ABDL MM Romance
Gifting Crayons: An ABDL MM Romance
One Kiss Less: A Sci-Fi MM Romance
No Turning Back: A Gay Arranged Marriage Romance
Just Say Yes: An Arranged Marriage M/M Romance
Against All Odds: A Gay Romance Bundle
Big Little Bundle: An ABDL MM Pet Play Collection
More than my Little: An ABDL MM Pet Play Bundle
Rub my Belly: An ABDL MM Pet Play Romance
Belly Rubbed: An ABDL MM Pet Play Romance
Colorful Littles: An ABDL MM Pet Play Bundle
Follow my Rules: An ABDL MM Pet Play Story
Collared Little: An ABDL MM Pet Play Story

ACKNOWLEDGEMENT

Designed by Wirestock - Freepik.com (cover).
Designed by Cookie_Studio - Freepik.com (cover).

ABOUT THE AUTHORS

Jerry Hastings

Jerry Hastings is a passionate gamer, an outspoken lover of his PS4, an advocate for minority rights, and a staunch supporter of the fight against homophobia. Much more than putting words on paper, his stories change people's lives and minds.

As a writer, his specialty is gay romance. His tales are spicier and more affectionate than those usually found elsewhere. Have your soothing tea ready, because his words will make your heart beat faster than it should.

Michael Levi

Michael Levi is a gay erotica author, although he does have some successful non m/m works in his collection. Knowing for hitting all the sweet spots of the reader and leaving everlasting impressions, his stories are not for those weak of the heart.

His works are perfect for readers looking for alpha males, bad boys, and tales with a touch of intimacy in every kiss. Michael Levi is known not just for telling a story, but also for exciting, engaging and arousing the reader.